High Seas

Doc's Study
At the Sunken Ship

Doc's
Lagoon

Island School

N
W · E
S

THE ADVENTURES OF
Blue Ocean Bob

A Journey Begins

To Paola (for sharing the journey) and
Nicolas (the captain of this ship) —B.A.O.

To Max (may you have many adventures) and
Jonah (watch out for whales!) —K.S.K.

The Adventures of

Blue Ocean Bob

A Journey Begins

by BROOKS OLBRYS

illustrated by KEVIN KEELE

Special thanks to Bob Proctor for his inspiration, Emma Walton Hamilton for her editorial guidance, and the dedicated crew at Greenleaf Book Group for preparing Blue Ocean Bob for the voyage.

Design and composition by Greenleaf Book Group LLC
Cover design by Greenleaf Book Group LLC
Illustrations by Kevin Keele

ISBN: 978-0-9829613-4-6

12 13 14   10 9 8 7 6 5 4 3 2 1
First Edition

Published by
Children's Success Unlimited LLC
521 Fifth Avenue, 27th Floor
New York, NY 10175

Printed in Singapore

Contents

⇒ Chapter 1 ⇐
Some Helpful Advice

There once was a boy who lived close to the sea
and daydreamed all day about what he might be.
His island was lush and his life wasn't bad,
but he wasn't content with the things that he had.

Bob said to himself, "I just know there is more.
This cannot be all that my life has in store!
Perhaps if I look for and find the right guide,
my days won't just ebb and flow with the tide."

His guardian, Xena, a blunt hummingbird,
was truly unsettled by what she had heard.
"Just where will you go, Bob? And what will you do?
Imagine the things that might happen to you!"

But Bob's mind was made up and he knew what was best.

So he stepped in his boat and set out on his quest.

"I'll ask the sea creatures if they can advise.

They seem to be generous, happy, and wise."

The first one he met was a dolphin named Al,

who lived a full life and was everyone's pal.

"What's your secret?" asked Bob, "You're so joyful and free!

Would you share your success and your knowledge with me?"

The dolphin just smiled. "Why, there's no secret in it!

I simply appreciate life's every minute.

For we are all given incredible power.

You have it right now, every day, every hour."

Young Bob was confused by the dolphin's suggestions.

It seemed that Al's answers just led to more questions.

"Perhaps you should visit my teacher instead,"

Al advised when he saw Bob was scratching his head.

"He's an elderly turtle and just goes by 'Doc.'

But sometimes we call him the Sage or the Rock."

Xena fluttered her wings and she squawked with dismay.

"I'm not sure we should venture quite so far away."

But Bob thanked the dolphin and headed due east.
He didn't heed Xena's alarms in the least.

He rowed with intent and arrived at the place
where Doc heard the sea creatures pleading their case
for why things should be better or what wasn't fair
or why life was hard and why Doc should care.

Now Doc, in his wisdom, had studied the greats

who had done brilliant things and determined their fates.

He had met with great whites, giant squids, and blue whales.

He had heard all their stories and read all their tales.

So Bob summoned courage and asked the old gent,

"Please tell me how to be truly content."

Doc tipped his spectacles, gave Bob a glance,
adjusted his shell and rebuckled his pants.

Then he said, "We've just met, but my instincts are sound,
and the answer you seek is quite easily found.
As Al may have told you, you have it within.
Discover your passion, then simply jump in.
Decide what you love, what excites and inspires,
then make that your purpose and watch what transpires."

Bob thought of the fish in the deep ocean blue
and the seabirds and sand crabs and jellyfish too.
As he pictured them all, he could feel his heart swell.
He knew what he loved, and he knew it quite well.

His passion was clear; he just had to pursue it.
Protecting all sea life—he knew he could do it.
"I'll simply devote all my days to the sea.
A marine biologist!" Bob declared. "Yes, that's me!"

"Oh, Doc, you're the best! You're so gracious and wise."

Then Doc spoke some words that took Bob by surprise.

"You are on your way, Bob, that's certainly clear,

but there is something more that I think you should hear.

Your purpose is set, but you're still far from through.

You'll face crooked pathways and challenges too.

So remember for each: Choose your thoughts, close your eyes.

Imagine your wish has come true—visualize!"

Bob took this to heart, shook Doc's flipper and said,

"Thank you, kind sir. There's a journey ahead!"

He picked up some clam shells, two oysters, a reed,

and he stuck them on top of his hat with seaweed.

"Come, Xena!" he cried. "I must get on the job!

The sea world awaits me! I'm Blue Ocean Bob!"

⇀≫ Chapter 2 ≪↼
A Clam Points the Way

Bob knew that his purpose, his reason to be,
was to care for all creatures and life in the sea.
But how to begin? Which direction to take?
There were so many possible choices to make!

Xena the hummingbird meant to assist,
but she worried a lot (though she tried to resist).
"What if you fail, Bob? Just what if you blow it?
This ocean's much bigger than you, and you know it!"
"Xena," Bob said, "It is true, I could fail.
But you can't leave the shore if you never set sail."

Bob thought, "It worked once, so it's sure to work twice.

I'll ask a sea creature or two for advice."

He wandered the beach and he spotted a clam.

"Excuse me," he said, "I'm in rather a jam.

I'm lucky because I've discovered my role,

but now I am stuck like a flag on a pole.

Is there a starting point you could suggest

to help me to care for the sea creatures best?"

"Yes, yes, yes," said the clam, a nice fellow named Earl.

"You want to learn how to create your own pearl!

Do you see this one here that I have in my shell?

Well, it didn't just happen (though that would be swell).

I came up with a strategy, followed a plan,

for fulfilling my aim to grow pearls out of sand.

"Finding your purpose is only the start.

Every good sailor must follow a chart.

So I'll tell you the next thing that you have to do:

Develop a vision and follow it through."

"What's a vision?" asked Bob. "Is it something I'll see?"

"It is more like a map to where you want to be.

And you'll need to stay flexible as you go forth.

You might swing east or west, but your vision is true north.

Though the path is rarely straight, to the vision be true,

for all that you seek is likewise seeking you.

"Now, Bob, would you do a small favor for me?
It may just reveal what your next step should be.
Mary Marine is at work on the pier.
Please take her this pearl that I promised last year."

"Gladly," said Bob. "I'll protect your pearl well."
And waving goodbye to the clam in his shell,
he rowed to the pier, where Miss Mary Marine
was feeding some baby sea turtles sardines.

"Greetings, I'm Bob. I was sent here by Earl.

Apparently you have a claim to this pearl?"

"Oh, yes!" Mary smiled. "It's a little bit late,

but the pearl is magnificent! Well worth the wait!

I work for the inn on this pier," Mary said.

"But I also make sure baby creatures are fed.

And then as they grow, I assist them with that,

like finding a shell for this crab who got fat.

Although marine science makes me content,

my job with the inn helps to pay for my rent."

Bob suddenly knew why the clam sent him here.

He needed a vision to make his path clear.

To develop this vision, his way through the maze,

he would research the sea creatures, study their ways!

But he'd need to get help from an expert, a pro.

Could that be Mary Marine? Maybe so . . .

⋅⋙ Chapter 3 ⋘⋅

A Chance Encounter

After his visit with Mary Marine,
Bob thought to tell Earl of the vision he'd seen:
to study the ocean and all of its creatures
with Mary as one of his mentors and teachers.

But as the tide started to ebb at its peak,
Bob noticed his boat had developed a leak.
He looked down and spotted a hole in the deck,
"S.O.S!" Xena shouted "Our vessel's a wreck!"
Then out from beneath the precarious craft
came a walrus, who looked at them both, and he laughed.
"I'm terribly sorry," he said, "that's the truth.
But I seem to have punctured your boat with my tooth."

"You can say that again!" Xena said with a shout.
"Just look at the damage you've done with that snout!"

Bob smiled at the walrus and put down his oar.

Then he asked him, quite calmly, to push them to shore.

The walrus—named Wallace—was glad to assist.

And knowing a chance like this shouldn't be missed,

Bob said, "Tell me, Wallace, from your point of view,

how can I succeed in a job that is new?"

Well, Wallace just chuckled, his eyes opened wide,
and he giggled and wiggled and jiggled his hide.
He said: "Bob, it's simple! As I like to say:
Don't just do things; do things a certain way."

"And what way is that?" Xena asked from the air.
"This walrus is not making sense, Bob. Beware!"

But Wallace ignored her (he'd heard that before)
and said as he scooted Bob's boat to the shore:

"Set a goal from your vision. And if you believe,
you might be surprised by what you can achieve.
Pinpoint your desire and keep it in mind.
Then act in the present, and soon you will find
that tomorrow's not here yet and yesterday's past.
So take action today like it may be your last.
And remember, stay calm and be confident too!
As you head for your goal, it will head toward you."

Well, Bob was amazed and gave Xena a wink.
A piece had been missing, but this was the link:
A purpose was crucial, a vision was key,
but a goal was the here and now of these three!

"Wallace," Bob said, "There's a girl on the pier.
I know my first goal! It is perfectly clear.
I'd like to assist her, learn all that she knows
about saving the sea life wherever she goes.
Whatever her need, whatever the role,
I'm ready to learn now that I've set my goal!"

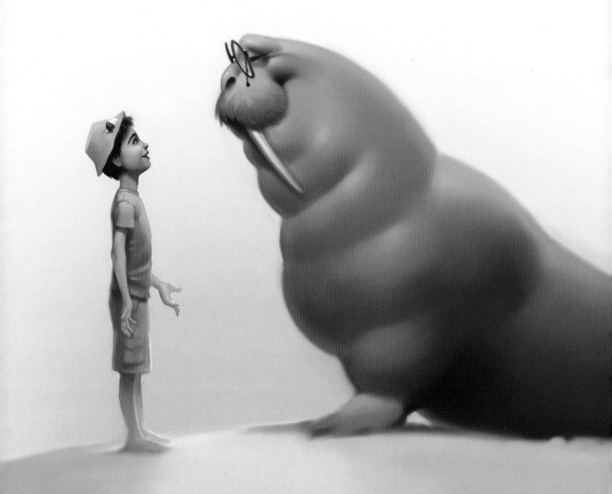

Then, leaving his rowboat and oars on the sand,

Bob set out on foot to give Mary a hand.

As he walked down the shore he heard Wallace's shout:

"A few final words, Bob, to help you, no doubt!

Don't forget! In this life, you are never alone.

You need not do everything all on your own.

With your purpose now set and your vision so clear,

you can act on your goals and watch wonders appear!"

⇶ Chapter 4 ⇷
The Magic Word

When Blue Ocean Bob went back to see Mary,
a job application seemed suddenly scary.
He paused at her door, and he felt his heart flutter.
Then Xena, his confidant, said with a mutter,
"Oh, Bob, you're not ready. You just do not know
what you will say to her, where it will go!
I suggest you delay it and take some time out.
You need to rethink this, clear up any doubt."

Her words struck a chord. What if Xena was right?
His vision might never take form or take flight.
But then Bob remembered old Doc's sage advice.
In order to "jump in," he shouldn't think twice.

So he went to the door and he gave it a tap,

and Mary came out with her satchel and cap.

She smiled, and before Bob could utter a word,

she said, "Welcome, Bob! Welcome, beautiful bird!"

"Thank you," Bob said. "I have come back to ask

if you might need help with a project or task.

I would like to assist with your maritime chores.

I have plenty of time and a boat with two oars."

"That's terrific!" said Mary, "But first, I suggest

a small but imperative attitude test.

I have here a sensor for Tom, the blue whale.

I'd like you to locate him, then tag his tail."

Bob thought of his boat in its leaky condition.
With no way to float, it was out of commission.
"I'll attempt to do what you've requested," he stated,
trying to hide that he felt so deflated.

"I told you!" said Xena. "You're too optimistic.
Your vision and plans are confused and simplistic.
And why did you say you had time and a boat?
You know very well that the thing doesn't float!"
"Xena, you're right." Bob said. "What was I thinking?
Just like our boat, now my dreams may be sinking."

With spirits so low, Bob set off down the shore.
And wouldn't you know it? It started to pour.

Then who should they meet in the sand but old Earl
working away on his next master pearl.
"Oh, Earl!" Bob exclaimed. "It's that Mary Marine.
She gave me a test I can't pass, it would seem.
She asked me to go out and tag a blue whale,
but my boat doesn't float; it will never set sail!"

"Ah, Bob," counseled Earl, "the answer my friend,
begins in your thoughts, but there does not end.
Your thoughts trigger feelings, which lead to your actions.
Then they set the stage for amazing reactions.
Think of the negative and you will fail.
Think of the positive? You'll tag that whale.
It's the magic word 'attitude,' which, if it's right,
will attract all the good that you have in your sight.
When you put it together, it's simple but true:
Your attitude shapes the world's image of you."

"Attitude, YES!" Bob's relief was immense.

Mary had said it—but now it made sense!

Then Bob had a feeling that came from a thought:

He might find a new way, as old Earl had taught.

He scanned the horizon over the sea

and spotted Al doing his flips, feeling free.

Bob yelled to the dolphin, "Hey Al, got a minute?

I now have a vision, and guess what? You're in it!"

"At your service!" said Al. "Let me know what you need.

I am here to assist you with vigor and speed."

So Bob waded out (Xena clung to his hat.)

He hopped on Al's back and they had a quick chat.

Then they turned toward the ocean and Al flipped his tail.

And would you believe it? Those three tagged that whale.

⇢❊ Chapter 5 ❊⇠
Persistence Pays Off

Bob was quite sure that he'd passed Mary's test.

He had tagged Tom at sea; even Xena was impressed!

So on their return when they filled Mary in,

they were startled to learn their real test would begin.

"Tom's been ill," Mary said, "and his strength has declined.

Please track him for thirty days; see what you find."

"Thirty days?" answered Xena. "How can we succeed?

Our boat's broken down and now Al's gone to feed!"

"Oh, Xena," said Mary, "that's just idle chatter!

If you know your true purpose, those facts do not matter."

Bob thought of his purpose; it seemed very clear:

help life in the sea and improve every year.

But to get on that path from the place he was now

would take someone like Mary to help show him how.

He made a decision to fix up his boat,

and track Tom the blue whale to places remote.

But reaching those places would not be a breeze,

for Bob hadn't captained his craft on high seas.

For ten days he tried, but with little success.

He rowed against waves, but was blocked by their crests.

His boat was pushed back, then got beached on the shore.

Now Bob felt more hopeless than ever before.

"Hello there!" called Earl, "Are you still on your quest?
I heard you were given a thirty-day test."

"Well, ten days have passed, so it seems I am through
with trying to do the things Mary can do."

"What nonsense!" said Earl. "You just misunderstood.
Your starting point's flexible; that's very good.
If you don't succeed in your first few forays,
don't give up, start anew, and go thirty more days!

"I suggest you see Doc—he's a pro on resistance.
I've learned from my pearls that the key is persistence.
For pearls take much longer than your current test—
Mary's pearl took five years, and may be my best."

"Thank you, Earl, you're terrific!" Bob gratefully said.

Then he rushed to see Doc, who was lounging in bed.

"Well, well, my good friends," chuckled Doc, somewhat groggy.

"Did Mary employ you? How'd you get so soggy?"

"She gave us a test, but I don't think it pays,

to track Tom the blue whale for thirty straight days.

The waves are too rough and my oars, only wood.

We can't reach the whale, though I hoped that we could."

Then Doc had an insight, as Earl had predicted.

He knew that Bob's goal and his mindset conflicted.

"Now, now, Bob and Xena, I'll give you a clue.

To track that blue whale, here is what you must do:

Don't focus on waves; they will bring you to shore.

Instead, picture deep sea where Tom was before.

It is true that those waves present major resistance,

but they are no match for your constant persistence.

If the dream you hold dear is as big as you say,

all the various obstacles have to give way."

"Persistence!" Bob nodded. "Earl mentioned it too!
I will go try again, and this time, follow through!"

Bob and Xena thanked Doc and they left for the beach
where they found their small boat, but Tom still out of reach.
Above them a seagull soared high in the sky,
sailing on currents of wind that came by.
It flew on those currents right out to the whale.
And Bob had a thought: "I should make my own sail!"

So Xena and he gathered palm leaves and wood,

and they built a big sail just as fast as they could.

Then Bob raised the sail on his boat and got in,

and he sailed to the place where that whale had last been.

They lost the whale twice. Xena squawked in alarm.

But persistence won out; the third time was the charm.

Then they tracked him for thirty days, watched him eat krill,

and returned to tell Mary: "Tom's no longer ill!"

Mary was pleased, but not really surprised,

for they'd done just as Doc and old Earl had advised.

Then she made Bob and Xena official assistants,

and said with a wink, "I know you'll go the distance!"

The Beginning . . .

To learn more about
The Adventures of Blue Ocean Bob™
and view other titles in the series,
please visit www.BlueOceanBob.com.

About The Author

As a lifelong student of achievement philosophies, Brooks Olbrys was inspired by his young son to make these philosophies accessible to children. With encouragement from best-selling author and personal development coach Bob Proctor, Brooks created the children's book series, The Adventures of Blue Ocean Bob.

A graduate of Stanford University, the Fletcher School of Law and Diplomacy at Tufts, and the University of California at Berkeley School of Law, Brooks is the founder of Children's Success Unlimited and a managing director at investment bank Ion Partners. He lives with his wife and son in New York City and greatly enjoys escapes to the North and South American coastlines.

About The Illustrator

From a young age, Kevin Keele has enjoyed creating artwork in many forms: drawing, oil painting, digital painting, even stained glass. His work has been featured in numerous picture books, magazines, board games, and video games. Though he lives far from any coastlines, he has always been fascinated by the ocean and enjoys illustrating its various creatures.

Kevin is currently an artist for Disney Interactive Studios. He lives in Utah with his wife and two sons. They're the caretakers of one grouchy cat, three chickens, and thousands of Italian honeybees.

Sea of
Kerchoo

Island of Roses

Inn up
on High